FEB 2 3 2004

P9-CQA-155

CONCEPT

CIRQUE DU SOLEIL ®

Parade of Colors

Written by Patrisha Robertson

xz
R

HARRY N. ABRAMS, INC., PUBLISHERS

Gathered here inside these pages
are colors galore
and rhymes for all ages!

Now, open your eyes!
Come look within!
For a parade of bright colors
is about to begin…

3

The Musicians

Boom di boom!
Twang twang!
Toot **toot!** Strum **ho!**

For our delight,
they start the show!

Look! Here they come!
Oh, there they go...

A symphony in WHITE.

The Singer in Black

Tra-la-la,
next comes the singer,
trilling high
and trolling low.

From tousled curls
to pointy toe,

The color she wears
is BLACK.

The Zebras

Oh me, oh my!
What's this? What's that?

Not one, not two, not merely a third,
but many together as a herd,

Dressed both in BLACK
and also WHITE,
so à la mode
and stripedly right...

(For zebras anyway...)

The Baron

La di dah!
Voilà!
The Baron!

BLACK and
WHITE
are the **colors** he loves.

But since he's dramatic
and somewhat **brash**,

He likes to add a
spicy **dash**
of RED!

Yao

Swish, swoosh,
a RED flag!

See it float, watch it fly!
Look how it shimmers
against the sky!

Is it a signal?
Or maybe a warning?
Or perhaps it's the way
Mr. Yao says,

"Good Morning!"

The Comet

On a YELLOW horse
and in
RED attire,

He's hot to trot,
his pace like fire!

But, splashity splish,
and splash away,
one thing, dear Comet,
I have to say…

Since water swirls
'round your hem
and your coat,

How come you didn't travel
…by boat?

Tamir
& Little Tamir

These two you see, dressed quite the same,
their relative stature denoted by **name**.

For while one's quite **big**,
the other's called **Little!**

(Tho' both stand straight as any **skittle**.)

And what else they share despite their sizes,
is...**oh crumbs**, no surprises...

A love for the color YELLOW!

Red Pierrot

Mr. RED Pierrot!
He's upside down!
An acrobat (and not a clown),

RED dressed with ORANGE
and happy that way...

For this is the way
he likes to stand:
tilted, balancing
on one hand.

Baroque
Le Dandy

Hi-dee-ho! Monsieur Le Dandy!

What makes your hair
stand up on end?
So stiffly stiff,
with no curl or bend?

Not blown about by breeze or sneeze,
but upright straight
as a Roman frieze!

Perhaps this 'do
keeps wisps off your face
as you leap about with
baroque-like grace...

Dapper in your suit of
fresh, clear ORANGE.

The Bronx

Oh yes!
Here are the Bronx!
A confident crew,

Decked out in GOLD
from helmet to shoe!

And though their
armor is quite rich,

It's scritchy-scratchy,
and makes 'em itch!

The Angels

They're angels!
       Good heavens!
I say, bless their noses!

They're rich, ruby RED
like the fanciest roses!

Do you think, like roses,
       they'll bloom and fade?
Or will these noses stay this shade?

La Garçonne

In a RED dress
she is skipping, skipping.
See how her hem
is flipping, flipping?

And in her hands
(so barely seen),
two handles bright,
of emerald GREEN.

Oops, lift your feet!
Yikes! Down you go…

No tripping, please!
Jump fast, then slow.

The Water Nymphs

A perfect balance!
GREEN on GREEN!

Don't teeter or totter.
Don't topple or fall.

Like blades of grass,
stand straight and tall!

Dreamer & Ringmaster

Close they sit, upon their chair,
looking quite odd, this mixed-up pair.

There's Dreamer who's snoozy
all dressed in BLUE.
Ringmaster's in YELLOW,
a shake-'n'-wake hue.

Though tones apart, they're often seen
combined to make a shade of GREEN.

(It's there in the cape — can you spot it?)

Quidam

How silently he stands,
his coat a turquoise BLUE,

Holding an **umbrella**
of much the same hue.

He can **walk** but not **talk**.
And there's no chance of **kissing**.

For his head is **not** there!
Look! See! It is missing!

The Nuts

Not at all **hairy!**
And hardly scary!

Smoothly **bald** and
BLUE of pate,
quite happy in
their **hairless** state.

Never to worry
'bout **brush or comb!**

(They can leave
those **safe** at home!)

21

The Palmtrees

Out of a PURPLE-BLUE mist,
these **tropical ladies**
float by...

Their skirts striped ORANGE
as orange peel,
silky and **lovely** to the feel.

And **fluttering** high,
and proud to be seen,
their **feathery** leaves of
shamrock GREEN.

The Mafioso

Oh, gee! Good golly! My gosh!

That tippity-slippity pole looks scary!

Though notice this guy's not
nervous or wary!

He's happy there, so high above,
all clad in a feathery PURPLE-y fuzz,

Enjoying his weebly wobbly berth,
until he slides BACK down to Earth.

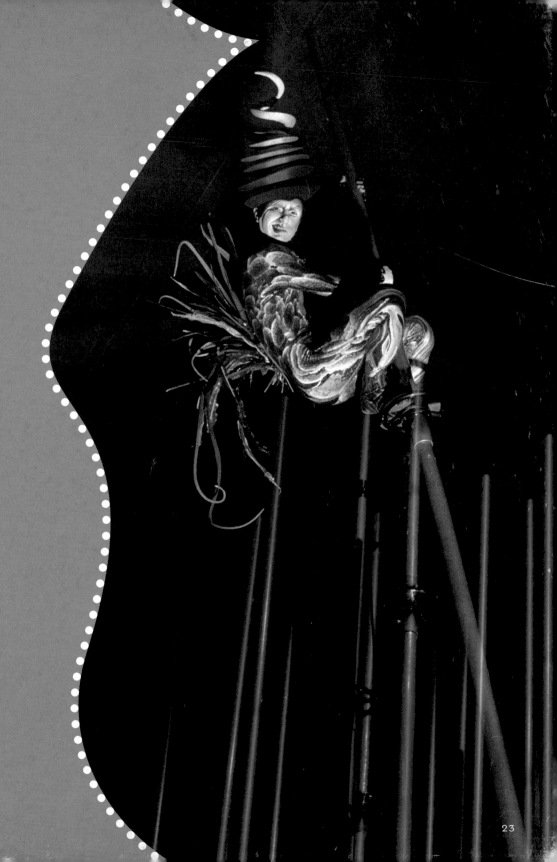

The Nostalgic Old Birds

Four friends of sorts, all garish and glitzy,
a razz-a-ma-tazz of sparkle—quite ritzy!

Though called, as they're named,
nostalgic and old,
their plumage is twinkling
with SILVER and GOLD...

With whiffles of PINK,
BLUE, YELLOW, and GREEN!
These birds of a feather are often seen
flocking together, exotic and flash.

(I wonder, my dear, can pale colors CLASH?)

The Urban Worms

Iggly, swiggly,
squiggle, and squish.
What a **thrashing**,
smashing dish!

A clamor of YELLOW,
GREEN, PINK,
and BLUE...

How **squirmy** to
meet you...
why how DO you do?

Now,
please **wriggle** on by...

Monsieur Fleur

Ooh-la-la Monsieur Fleur!
So florally fabulous (full of allure...)

RED coat! BLUE vest!
And check out your hat,
it must be your best!
We've no doubt about that!

Bowl-like and rounded, just as a bud.
Though as flower shades go,
it's a bit of a dud!

For blossoming on your flashy tip-topper,
is a shade of fleur not quite so proper...

Defiantly planted, of color askew,
this hat blooms in bat-BLACK...
(an unflowery, dark hue!)

The Baroques

RED hot! And popping PINK!
Such dynamos of their hues!

The Baroques are rash,
and they love to clash...

(With each other, of course,
not you!)

Oh BOO! OH HOO! We're off...away!
Ta-Ta! Adieu! We cannot stay.

But though we bid our last goodbye,
what lingers behind—and will not fly?

This parade of colors you have seen:
YELLOW, PURPLE, PINK, and GREEN.

ORANGE, BLACK, WHITE, RED, and BLUE...
a vibrant cast of shade and hue!

Performing beyond this book of rhyme,
these colors exist throughout all time...

High-flying. Fantastic! Juggling good cheer!
How nice to think you met them here!

Splashy and bright! And beautifully blending,
a brilliant act that's never-ending!

(Toodle-oo!)

Notes

Renowned for its innovative blend of circus arts and street performance, Cirque du Soleil has been captivating audiences around the world since 1984.

Cirque du Soleil began with a very simple dream: a group of young entertainers got together to perform, see the world, and have fun! Every year audiences get bigger and bigger as Cirque continues to discover new places and new ideas. And they're still having fun!

Today Cirque du Soleil continues to dream of enriching the lives of all those who cross its path. Through its actions and creativity, Cirque hopes to imbue new projects with the energy and inspiration that are the essence of its shows. Cirque du Soleil especially wants to help young people express and realize their dreams. As Cirque heads into the future, projects like *Parade of Colors* will allow it to share its vision in a whole new way.

We hope you'll be inspired to dream your own dreams, and to believe that they, too, can come true.

Credits

Photographs on the front cover and on pages 4–5, 7, 10–11, 14–15, 24, and 26:
Alegría®
Creative team: Director, Franco Dragone; Director of Creation, Gilles Ste-Croix; Choreographer, Debra Brown; Lighting Designer, Luc Lafortune; Set Designer, Michel Crête; Sound Designer, Guy Desrochers; Costume Designer, Dominique Lemieux; Composer and Musical Director, René Dupéré; Make-Up Designer, Nathalie Gagné.

Photos: Al Seib
Photographs © 1994, 1999, 2001 Cirque du Soleil Inc.

Photographs on the back cover and on pages 2–3, 7, 13, 18–19, 25, and 27:
Saltimbanco®
Creative team: Director, Franco Dragone; Director of Creation, Gilles Ste-Croix; Choreographer, Debra Brown; Lighting Designer, Luc Lafortune; Set Designer, Michel Crête; Sound Designer, Jonathan Deans; Costume Designer, Dominique Lemieux; Composer and Musical Director, René Dupéré; Make-Up Designers, Jean Bégin and Nathalie Gagné.

Photos: Al Seib
Photographs © 1995, 1999, 2002 Cirque du Soleil Inc.

Photographs on pages 6, 9, and 28–29:
"O"™
Creative team: Writer and Director, Franco Dragone; Director of Creation, Gilles Ste-Croix; Choreographer, Debra Brown; Lighting Designer, Luc Lafortune; Set Designer, Michel Crête; Sound Designers, François Bergeron and Jonathan Deans; Costume Designer, Dominique Lemieux; Composer and Musical Director, Benoît Jutras; Make-Up Designer, Nathalie Gagné.

Photos: Véronique Vial
Photographs © 1998 Cirque du Soleil Inc.

Photographs on pages 8 and 17:
Dralion™
Creative team: Director, Guy Caron; Director of Creation, Gilles Ste-Croix; Choreographer, Julie Lachance; Lighting Designer, Luc Lafortune; Set Designer, Stéphane Roy; Sound Designer, Guy Desrochers; Costume Designer, François Barbeau; Composer and Musical Director, Violaine Corradi; Make-Up Designer, Yves Le Blanc

Photos: Al Seib
Photographs © 2000, 2002, 2003 Cirque du Soleil Inc.

Photographs on pages 12 and 21:
La Nouba™
Creative team: Writer and Director, Franco Dragone; Director of Creation, Gilles Ste-Croix; Choreographer, Debra Brown; Lighting Designer, Luc Lafortune; Set Designer, Michel Crête; Sound Designers, François Bergeron and Jonathan Deans; Costume Designer, Dominique Lemieux; Composer and Musical Director, Benoît Jutras; Make-Up Designer, Nathalie Gagné.

Photos: Véronique Vial and Jean-François Gratton
Photographs © 1998, 2002 Cirque du Soleil Inc.

Photographs on pages 16 and 20:
Quidam®
Creative team: Director, Franco Dragone; Director of Creation, Gilles Ste-Croix; Choreographer, Debra Brown; Lighting Designer, Luc Lafortune; Set Designer, Michel Crête; Sound Designer, François Bergeron; Costume Designer, Dominique Lemieux; Composer and Musical Director, Benoît Jutras; Make-Up Designer, Nathalie Gagné.

Photos: Al Seib
Photographs © 2002 Cirque du Soleil Inc.

Photograph on page 22:
Mystère®
Creative team: Director, Franco Dragone; Director of Creation, Gilles Ste-Croix; Choreographer, Debra Brown; Lighting Designer, Luc Lafortune; Set Designer, Michel Crête; Sound Designer, Jonathan Deans; Costume Designer, Dominique Lemieux; Composers and Arrangers, René Dupéré and Benoît Jutras; Make-Up and Mask Designers, Angelo Barsetti, Nathalie Gagné, and Richard Morin.

Photos: Al Seib
Photographs © 2002 Cirque du Soleil Inc.

Photograph from page 23:
Varekai™
Creative team: Writer and Director, Dominic Champagne; Director of Creation, Andrew Watson; Choreographers, Michael Montanaro and Bill Shannon; Lighting Designers, Nol van Genuchten and Luc Lafortune; Set Designer, Stéphane Roy; Sound Designer, François Bergeron; Costume Designer, Eiko Ishioka; Composer and Musical Director, Violaine Corradi; Projection Designer, Francis Laporte; Rigging Designer, Jaque Paquin; Make-Up Designer, Nathalie Gagné.

Photos: Véronique Vial
Photographs © 2002 Cirque du Soleil Inc.

Text dedicated to Marion M. Robertson ("Mum")...
and to all those who make my life a dance.
— P.R.

Designer: Allison Henry

Cirque du Soleil, *Quidam*, *Dralion*, and *Varekai* are trademarks of Créations Méandres Inc. in Canada and Japan,
and of The Dream Merchant Company Kft. elsewhere in the world and are used under license.
Saltimbanco and *Alegría* are trademarks of Créations Méandres Inc. in Canada, Japan, and the United States,
and of The Dream Merchant Company Kft. elsewhere in the world and are used under license.
Mystère, *La Nouba*, and "O" are trademarks of Créations Méandres Inc. and are used under license.

Library of Congress Cataloging-in-Publication Data

Seib, Al.
Cirque du Soleil : a parade of colors / photographs by Al Seib, Véronique Vial, and Jean-François Gratton;
Written by Patrisha Grainger Robertson.
p. cm.
Summary: Characters from the circus troupe Cirque du Soleil celebrate
the colors of the rainbow.
ISBN 0-8109-4515-0
[1. Color—Fiction. 2. Cirque du Soleil—Fiction. 3. Circus—Fiction.
4. Stories in rhyme.] I. Robertson, Patrisha Grainger. II. Title.

PZ8.3.S455Ci 2003
[E]—dc21
2003003830

Published in 2003 by Harry N. Abrams, Incorporated, New York

Printed in China
10 9 8 7 6 5 4 3 2 1

Harry N. Abrams, Inc.
100 Fifth Avenue
New York, N.Y. 10011
www.abramsbooks.com

Abrams is a subsidiary of